Buttons' Bouquet

by Lynn Groth

illustrated by Tammie Lyon

NORTHWESTERN PUBLISHING HOUSE
Milwaukee, Wisconsin

Special thanks to Paul Burmeister for his art and story direction.

Library of Congress Control Number: 2002100800
Northwestern Publishing House
1250 N. 113th St., Milwaukee, WI 53226-3284
© 2003 Northwestern Publishing House
www.nph.net
Published 2003
Printed in the United States of America
ISBN 0-8100-1334-7

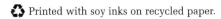 Printed with soy inks on recycled paper.

Buttons is a little bear
Who's growing, just like you.
He wants to learn so many things.
And you can learn them too!

As you turn each page, please look—
A button may hide there.
And listen as the story tells
About God's love and care.

Be kind . . . to one another.

Ephesians 4:32

Buttons burst into the kitchen. "Momma, look!" he shouted. "I found a dollar! Now can I buy the super red car with doors that open and close?"

In Buttons' hand was a wet, crumpled dollar bill that he had found outside in the grass.

"Let's see," said Mother. "Yes, this dollar with the other money you have saved should be enough to buy your car." As she said this, she quietly tucked a little box into her pocket.

"Super!" said Buttons.

His mother said, "It's not super that someone lost the money, Buttons, but if someone had to find it, I'm glad it was you."

"Me too! Let's go buy my car," answered Buttons.

"First I must finish making soup and cookies," said Mother.

"Cookies? Super!" said Buttons. "May I have some?"

"Only two," she said. "We'll take the rest of the cookies and all the soup to Mrs. Cozy."

"Ohhh! Why are you giving away our food?" asked Buttons. "I like soup too."

"Buttons, we have plenty of food. Mrs. Cozy doesn't have much money to buy food. And she's sick. Why don't you go pick a bouquet of flowers for Mrs. Cozy? You can go to her house with me and give them to her."

"Awww," said Buttons between bites of cookie. "I don't want
to. I want to go buy my car."

Hmmm . . . thought Mother.

She turned off the stove and said, "Buttons, Jesus wants us to be kind and helpful to others. That's how we show thanks to Jesus for dying on the cross to take away our sins. Let me tell you a Bible story about a kind woman named Tabitha."

Tabitha showed love to Jesus by showing love and kindness to others. Tabitha helped poor people. She made robes and other kinds of clothing for them.

But one day Tabitha became very sick and died. Her friends were very sad. They missed Tabitha.

One of Jesus' friends heard that Tabitha had died. That friend was Peter. He went to the house where she lay dead. Some friends of Tabitha told Peter, "Look at the clothing Tabitha made for other people before she died."

Peter looked at the clothing, and then he sent the friends out of the room.

Peter kneeled on the floor and prayed, because he knew that only Jesus has the power to help.

Peter looked at the dead woman and said, "Tabitha, get up."

He took her hand and helped her stand.

Then Peter called the friends back into the room to see Tabitha. The power of Jesus had made her come alive!

After Mother finished telling the Bible story, she said, "I think Tabitha probably kept making clothes for the poor. She showed love to Jesus by helping people."

Buttons thought about the kind things Tabitha had done. He wanted to show love to Jesus by doing kind things too.

Then he ran outside to the flower garden. Buttons picked one flower of each color—yellow, pink, blue, white, and purple.

Mother gave Buttons a vase to hold the flowers. Then she and Buttons walked across the street to Mrs. Cozy's house.

Mrs. Cozy was happy to have visitors. She said, "The soup and cookies smell very good. And so do your flowers, Buttons."

She sniffed one flower at a time—yellow, pink, blue, white—
and then she stopped.

Inside the purple flower was a rolled-up dollar bill. "Why, I've never seen a flower like this one. Thank you," said Mrs. Cozy.

"You're welcome, Mrs. Cozy," said Buttons. "I hope you feel better soon."

Mother smiled and put her hand on Buttons' shoulder as
they walked back home. "Thank you," she said, "for cheering up
Mrs. Cozy."

"Here is a surprise I have been saving for you." She took the little box from her pocket.

"Super!" said Buttons.

He carefully opened the box. "My red car!" he shouted. "Thank you! What a super surprise!"

And sure enough, Buttons could open and close every door on the car.

Did you find the buttons
That were hiding here and there?
Someone special has found you.
He gives you love and care.

Jesus is that someone's name.
He lived and died for you.
Trust him, love him, and obey
In all you say and do.